MISSION TO MARATHON

MISSION TO MARATHON

GEOFFREY TREASE

A & C Black • London

This edition 2006
First published 1997 in hardback by
A & C Black Publishers Ltd
38 Soho Square, London, W1D 3HB

www.acblack.com

Text copyright © 1997 Geoffrey Trease

The right of Geoffrey Trease to be identified as the
author of this work has been asserted by him in accordance
with the Copyrights, Designs and Patents Act 1988.

ISBN 0-7136-7677-9
ISBN 978-0-713-67677-8

A CIP catalogue for this book is available from the British Library.

A & C Black uses paper produced with elemental chlorine-free
pulp, harvested from managed sustained forests.

Printed and bound in Great Britain by Bookmarque Ltd, Croydon

Contents

1

The Persians Are Coming

'Is that you, Philip?'

Father sounded impatient. Philip hurried into the workshop.

'I'm here, Father.'

'Where on earth have you been?'

'Only school.' Philip was puzzled. Where else could he have been?

His father faced him, hammer and chisel in hand. The floor was littered with marble chippings. 'Dawdling along with your school friends, I suppose?'

Father was really the kindest of men. But he was also Lycon, one of the best sculptors in Athens. Any artist could get impatient when his mind was full of the work in hand.

Philip had not dawdled. In fact he had

hurried home. Some of the men in the street looked so worried. They were talking in low tones. He had felt a tension in the air.

He pointed to the shadow at his feet, cast by the sunshine slanting through the doorway. The workshop faced south. That shadow might be short or long, according to the season or the time of day. But its angle proved whether you were late or early.

It now stretched roughly along the line it usually did when he returned from school.

'I'm sorry,' said Father. 'I was so anxious to get on with the statue. I've done so little work of any kind today. There was a sudden meeting of the Assembly. I had to go.'

Every citizen was expected to attend. They had to stream out to a little rocky hill, the Pnyx, on the west side of the city, crowding its slopes in their thousands. Every man had the right to speak in the debate if he wanted to. Every man had a vote. Father was not much interested in politics but he had to be there.

Was this why the passers-by had been looking so anxious? Philip wanted to ask, but he knew better.

'Now you're here,' said Father, 'I can get back to the statue. It's that left arm. The muscles.'

Philip was his model for the young god Pan, the protector of shepherds, who led the nymphs dancing over the mountains to the music of his pipes. He was worshipped all over Greece but not so much by the townsfolk of Athens. His father had been delighted when a rich man ordered a statue of Pan. The shepherds' god, half boy, half goat, made a change from the more dignified gods and goddesses.

Philip jumped up on the slab of stone they used as a pedestal, threw aside the knee-length tunic which was all he wore, and picked up his pipes, which he had made with reeds corded together and waxed. He raised them to his lips as if about to play.

'An inch or two higher,' his father ordered.

It was a tiring pose. Father gave him occasional rests but he seemed anxious to get on. The tightened muscles showed in the uplifted arms.

'I must get them just right,' he said. So many statues were so stiff and solid.

He always tried to get life and warmth into them – even in marble.

At last Father seemed satisfied. 'That will do. I had to get this done today. I shall not have your services tomorrow.'

'Why not?' asked Philip in amazement. He stepped down and put on his tunic.

'You will not be here, my boy. Let me explain. As we heard a day or two ago, the Persians have got as far as Euboea.'

Philip nodded, listening eagerly. Euboea was dangerously close. It was the long narrow island stretching down the eastern coast of mainland Greece, separated from it by a thin strait of sea. So the Persians were now as near as that! No wonder the people in the streets were looking scared.

He had heard a lot about the Persians. Their Darius – who was known as the Great King – ruled over a vast empire. It now extended far beyond Persia itself and came down to the shores of Asia, facing Greece across the Aegean Sea.

'We were told at the Assembly today,' his father went on, 'that their expedition has conquered Euboea. They have plundered the temples and burnt them down. They are deporting the people into slavery—'

'*No!*'

'Yes,' said his father firmly. 'And now, we learn, they are crossing over to the mainland. The Great King is determined to teach Athens a lesson. But his armies are not likely to sail straight across to us here.'

The invasion forces would choose a place where they could land without opposition, have good anchorage for their hundreds of ships and find a level plain – so rare amid the mountains of Greece – where they could use the splendid cavalry of which they were so proud.

'So,' Father concluded, 'the Bay of Marathon is an obvious choice.'

'*Marathon?*' Philip's eyes almost started out of his head. What about his grandmother? And his aunt?

'Won't everybody be in danger?' he asked.

'Exactly. That is why you will not be here with me tomorrow.'

2

Job For a Boy

The family talked over the whole situation as they ate their meal.

It was a good solid one. A tasty mutton broth. They seldom had meat. More often it was fish.

'But I thought we'd better build our strength up,' said Mother grimly. 'Only the gods know what lies ahead.'

Father's elder brother, Nearchus, had the old family farm overlooking the sea at Marathon. Their mother lived on in the old home. They would all be in terrible danger if the Persians came ashore there. But whereas everyone else, if worst came to worst, could take to the hills, Philip's grandmother was now too frail for that.

'We must get her down here to us – if she is fit to travel at all,' Mother agreed. 'And the sooner we get the warning to them the better.'

Philip's elder brothers, Lucius and Callias, were old enough for military service and had been given their standby orders that afternoon.

Philip had made the journey countless times throughout his childhood, but never alone. It was about 25 miles by the usual route. A little shorter if you cut across the mountains by the higher way, but it was naturally steeper and rougher underfoot.

'I hope he'll be all right,' said Mother doubtfully.

Philip hoped so too, but secretly. Aloud he said, confident and a little cross, 'Course I shall! I could find my way there with my eyes shut.'

'Well, don't try,' ordered his father. 'We don't want you to break your neck.' He raised his hand to quell Philip's protest. 'You can't do it in the day, even if you run some of it. Your legs just aren't long enough. That's not your fault. When it gets towards dusk look round for some sheltered corner where you can curl up and get a few hours' sleep.' He laughed at the look on Philip's face. 'You think you *won't* sleep? You'll see, lad, after all those miles. Then, at first light, you'll be dropping down to the farm just as they're starting their day's work.'

After the meal Philip helped his brothers clean their armour for tomorrow's parade. He felt envious. The bronze metal took on such a superb polish. But, he reminded himself, he could not help being too young to fight in battles. After all, he reminded himself proudly, he was being trusted with this vital and possibly dangerous mission across the mountains.

Both his brothers were tall and strong, so they were in the heavy infantry. That meant a crested helmet with a narrow nosepiece and good protection for cheeks and ears. The helmet was lined with leather inside.

For the body there was a breastplate moulded to the shape of a man's chest, and another to go over his back, the two pieces joined together by leather straps. From kneecap to ankle, the soldier had greaves.

For further protection he carried a round or oval shield on his left arm. It was made of leather and wood, with metal plates. One of Father's friends was a clever painter and he had decorated the shield of Lucius with a very fierce-looking porcupine. For Callias he had gone one better.

He had painted a Gorgon's head. Gorgons were hideous mythical monsters who grew snakes instead of hair. The mere sight of them could turn a man to stone.

Philip hoped the shield would have this effect on any Persian who tried to harm his brother. But he didn't have much confidence in it. Such stories came from long ago.

Athens could muster only about ten thousand armoured infantry. What was that against the countless hordes the Great King could send over from his Persian Empire?

The trouble was, Greece was not only a much smaller country but it wasn't a single united country, ruled by one government. It was divided up, every big city on its own – Athens, Corinth, Thebes, and so on. They were all Greeks, but were often jealous of each other and would even fight wars.

Surely, at a time of crisis like this, they ought to stand together and face the Persians with a united front?

'They will,' Lucius assured Philip. 'It was agreed today at the Assembly. We are sending an urgent appeal to the Spartans. The Spartans are marvellous fighters. *They'll* come and help us.'

'Will the message get to them in time?'

Philip knew that Sparta was a long way off. About 140 miles.

'It should. They're giving it to Pheidippides to take.'

'Oh *good*!' Philip was much relieved. He knew that name – that of the finest runner in Athens. He had won trophies at the last Olympic Games. Who could cover the ground faster than he could?

'And the Spartans won't waste time when they get it,' said Callias. Even in their armour the Spartans could do forced marches at incredible speed.

Philip felt happier. Other cities would follow a lead from Sparta. Troops would soon be streaming in from every corner of Greece.

'Hadn't you better get some sleep?' Callias reminded him. 'Marathon is not as far away as Sparta – but you haven't such long legs as Pheidippides.'

3

Over the Hills

Philip set off at dawn. Now the moment had come, he was really keyed up at the thought of the responsibility laid upon him.

His mother tried to sound matter-of-fact but he guessed that she too was anxious. She insisted that he took a short cloak, fastened with a brooch under his chin. Though it was still September it would be chilly after nightfall, especially in the high hills. His linen tunic wouldn't stretch to cover his legs.

'And remember, you won't be walking – let alone running – once it's dark. You must find some sheltered corner out of the wind.'

She handed him a little package. Dried figs and raisins, bread and his favourite honey cakes.

'If you lose your way these will set you right.'

'They should!' He laughed. The honey came from his uncle's hives, it should have given the cakes the same homing instinct as the bees who had made it.

Old Davus walked with him for the first mile, to see him out of town and make sure he took the right route.

This was like old times. Davus had always taken him to school when he was little. Most of the younger boys were escorted by a family slave.

That was what Davus was, though Philip always thought of him as a friend.

He was the only slave they had. Many people had none, but a sculptor needed a strong helper for handling the massive lumps of marble or other stone he had to shape into beautiful figures.

So, years before Philip was even born, his father had bought Davus from the silver mines at Laurium, where he had been toiling away under terrible conditions. 'He saved my life,' Davus would often say. 'Men did not last long in those infernal mines.'

In Athens, a slave's life wasn't too hard, unless he was in mining or a galley slave straining at a heavy oar. A few were in small workshops, helping a craftsman such as a carpenter or potter. If trade was bad they couldn't be sacked like free men. They were always sure of their food. Most – the women especially – did housework.

'The Spartans sneer at you,' said Davus. 'They say that in the streets of Athens you can't see the difference between a free man and a slave.'

'I think our way's better,' said Philip.

'The Spartans are harsh masters,' Davus admitted, 'but they are the finest soldiers in Greece.'

That morning Philip was thinking a good deal about that, hoping that the runner would soon arrive in Sparta and that help would be quickly on the way. How could the Athenians beat the Persians on their own? What would happen if those barbarian hordes overwhelmed them? Would the Persians do what they seemed to be doing to the islanders of Euboea – carry off all the population into slavery?

He shuddered at the thought. It would be very different from being a slave in Athens.

The last houses were behind them. 'I must go back now,' said Davus. 'I have to take a message to your schoolmaster – your father is sending an apology, explaining why you will be absent for a few days.' He pointed to the track leading steeply up into the hills. 'This is the way you must go. Don't get lost.'

'I shan't,' Philip assured him. He quickened his pace as they parted. He wanted to show that he could get to Marathon much faster than Davus could have done.

After a little while he looked back. Davus was plodding his way back at the leisurely speed of an old man. He was just vanishing into the outskirts of the city.

Would that low ground soon become a battlefield, with his brothers standing shoulder to shoulder, their heavy spears levelled against the wild charge of the famous Persian cavalry? He tried to push such thoughts out of his head. He could not.

What would happen if the sheer weight of enemy numbers smashed through the

Athenian line? His brothers – and all their comrades – would never run away. They would fight their way backwards, yard by yard, to the Acropolis, the hill on which the city had been founded, and where all the women and children would have taken refuge already.

He stared at that hill now. It rose steeply in sheer precipices, flat-topped – big enough until recent years to carry almost the whole city. It was only on one side that the cliff was broken enough for people to walk up and down.

The Persians would have a job to fight their way up. With any luck they could be held at bay until the Spartans and other Greek forces arrived. His mother, grandmother, and other members of the family he could bring back from Marathon, would be saved.

He never forgot the view that morning. It was the smaller city he had known as a boy. Only when he was an old man did he see it in all its later glory, with the great white marble temple of the Parthenon, countless other new buildings, and the famous Long Walls that would keep out future invaders.

Today, though, all that mattered was to get to his uncle's and deliver his message. Speed was vital. He could go faster without the old man. He turned northwards, lengthened his stride and made for the skyline. The morning sun was on his shoulders now, growing all the time in strength.

Nobody else seemed to be using this upland route today. He saw two solitary shepherds, not near enough to speak to. He waved and they waved back. One other he came face to face with, at a stream where he had paused for a drink. At this time of year so many of the mountain streams were dried up. He was glad to find an ice-cold spring bubbling up out of the hillside.

He asked the stranger if he had heard any news of the Persians. The man had not and didn't seem worried.

'They won't come up here,' he said. 'What is there?'

He didn't even know that they were in Euboea. From where they were standing they could see a great expanse of sea stretching away eastwards to Asia. The long crinkly island of Euboea lay almost at their feet. Only that narrow blue channel separated them from the dreaded barbarians.

Philip continued his journey. It had been good to break the silence for a few moments.

He broke it again when his mind turned to school and he guessed that about now they would be reciting the lines of poetry they had all been learning by heart. To test his own memory Philip declaimed them as he strode forward through the solitary hills.

Their teacher was great on Homer, the blind poet who long ago had made up that exciting poem, the *Iliad*, about the siege of Troy. Philip loved it too – the lines rolled off the tongue. It was the best thing about school, after the games and the gymnastics. Much better than the geometry and the arithmetic.

He ran out of breath before he ran out of Homer. That up-and-down path, often steep and rough, wasn't ideal for reciting. The hills became silent again.

School must have finished by now. His shadow no longer jumped and wavered in front of him. It was getting longer too. Then he couldn't see it at all. The sun was in his eyes. In a few hours there would be no sun at all.

His legs ached, he was slowing down. He found himself stopping more and more often. He nibbled hungrily at one of the dried figs. He'd better not gobble up all the honey cakes. Keep them for the night – and first thing in the morning.

It would be wonderful to get to his aunt's. She always had something for a ravenous boy. If only he could have got there tonight! Less and less did he fancy a night on this desolate mountainside. He bit his lip and tried to hurry. Could he do it, after all? It didn't take long to discover that he certainly couldn't.

What was there to be afraid of? Nothing, surely. But never in his life, waking or sleeping, would he have been entirely alone for so many hours.

The sheep and the goats didn't count. You couldn't talk to *them*. It was getting unlikely now that he would meet another human being. Human beings, no – but there were other beings, weren't there – that might rove the hills at the dead of night?

Monsters, like the Gorgon painted on his brother's shield... Or Pan, the real god himself, whom he had dared to model for in his father's studio... Terrible stories came back to him of people who had encountered the god in some wild solitary place like this. It had been a terrifying experience. The true Pan had been quite different from what they had imagined. No smiling youth, capering about gaily on his shaggy goat legs, playing his pipes and leading lovely nymphs in their dances.

There was a special word for the crazy terror that could seize people if they met the real god. The word was panic.

It was his own fault, Philip had to admit, for choosing this upland route to his uncle's, just to save a mile or two. He had to face the unwelcome fact now – he was not going to make it tonight. He must be high up on

Mount Pentelicus now. He had often stared up at these massive heights from the farm so far below.

'I get my best marble from Pentelicus,' Father used to say. The block from which Philip's statue was now being chiselled must have come from near here. It might have been dragged on a sledge along one of these paved tracks the workmen made to ease their task of getting such weights down to the plain.

In the failing light he saw one of the quarries ahead. Fine! It would give him shelter overnight from the cool breeze blowing up from the bay. And there was clean water splashing down the rock face from a convenient spring above.

He chose a corner, ate his last honey cake but one, and stretched out on the hard ground, muffled in his cloak and wishing it was longer. He did not expect sleep to come easily, but it did. Never before in his young life had he walked so many miles in a single day.

At first it was a heavy, exhausted sleep, untroubled by dreams. But at last came the moment he had come to fear. Pan! The god was actually coming towards him. Playing his pipes—

Philip woke with a gasp of horror. It was daylight again. It seemed that the dawn, like a pink and gold tapestry, was being drawn up out of the sea.

It had not been a dream, for the pipes went on. Real footsteps were approaching. Light ones, but human. Not the click of goat hoofs.

There was a patter too, then a flurry of hot breath, a cold wet nose against his face. Welcoming him.

The dog knew him, he knew the dog. Argus, named after the dog in Homer. And here was his cousin herself. 'Nycilla!' he cried, delighted and deeply relieved.

She was clearly feeling the same. She had stopped in her tracks at the sight of a huddled stranger on the ground. Now she rushed forward and hugged him as he scrambled to his feet. Argus danced round them, barking in ecstasy.

4

Where to Hide?

Breathless, Philip explained why he was there. After those first minutes of delighted greeting the grim reality of his mission came flooding back.

'The Persians?' Nycilla cried in alarm. 'We've heard rumours, of course. What's been happening over in Euboea. Some men came over – they'd escaped – they told people in the village. Awful stories. But nothing about the Persians coming here themselves.'

'They wouldn't know. Why should they?'

'But why should the Persians come here? There's nothing! Only our little village and two or three others.'

'It's a place to land. A place where they can

moor all their galleys. And their supply ships. Where else, around here?'

'I see.' She knitted her brows. 'We'd better get back – find Father. You must be hungry. We'll get you some food.'

He did not say 'no'. She had already checked that the sheep were all right. They started briskly along the path.

'How *is* Grandmother?' he asked.

'Not so well.'

'Could she manage the journey to Athens? My father says—'

'We'll have to see.' Nycilla sounded gloomy. 'Perhaps the Persians *won't* come this way.'

To lighten the conversation he made her laugh. He told her how he had been wakened, and frightened for a moment by the sound of her pipes, and why the shepherds' god had been so much in his mind lately.

'Uncle Lycon will be missing you,' she said. 'All because of us!'

'Because of the Persians, you mean,' he reassured her.

'Anyhow his work will be at a standstill.'

'Not unless something else has cropped up. Remember – Pan's half goat. Father doesn't need my lower half. He's going to borrow a goat.' He laughed. 'It won't keep as still as I do.' The goat's shaggy legs would be a problem too. It needed all a sculptor's skill to represent soft hair in hard stone. That goat would keep Father fully occupied.

'You must feel proud to be a statue – even half of you!' She sounded wistful.

'If we get to Athens,' he said quickly, 'Father will pounce on *you*. It's some time since he saw you. I think he'll say you've grown up into a real young nymph.'

'You mean that?' She was clearly delighted. 'Even with all this hair? And marble so hard?'

'He'll find your head worth the trouble. More than a goat's hindquarters!'

They hurried on, laughing. They had to walk in single file now. The track was zigzagging down into a steep-sided valley. At the bottom flowed the Charadra – hardly flowing today, little more than a dried-up watercourse on this September day, though in another month or two it would be a furious mountain torrent.

The houses of Marathon village were strung along its banks. Philip's uncle lived in one of the first they came to, his land spread across the head of the valley.

'There's Father,' cried Nycilla. She called and waved. Nearchus stood up, shading his eyes with his hand. He shouted back, a shout of deep-voiced surprise from the depths of his black beard.

'Not *Philip*?'

'Yes, Uncle!'

Philip broke into a run, shooting past his cousin, loose pebbles flying from under his feet.

His uncle had been busy among the vines. Nearchus was always busy with something. It was a small family farm. No slaves, just sons and daughters, and two or three poorer neighbours with no land of their own to work on it.

As the months of the year went round the little patches of almost-level ground had to be ploughed, and sown with barley, and harvested. The olive trees must be pelted with stones to make them drop their fruit. The vine terraces must be pruned, the grapes gathered and laid out like the figs and olives to dry in the sun, or trodden with well-washed feet to make juice for the new season's wine. There were beans and peas to pick, combs of honey to remove – oh, so carefully! – from the hives. Goats to be milked, eggs collected.

If the farm didn't produce something you didn't have it.

'You have walked all the way? By yourself?' said Uncle. 'You must be ravenous!' He turned to his daughter. 'Run on, my dear. Tell your mother. This poor lad!'

'Father sent me to warn you. They say the Persians will choose Marathon as a landing place.' Philip stammered out his urgent message. His uncle's face clouded as Nycilla's had done. The girl sped off.

'I don't know, I don't know at all. We must consider it. It could be the death of your grandmother, a journey like that.'

He hadn't realised that the Persian invaders might come across the straits from

Euboea. But he took the warning very seriously. He had great respect for his younger brother in Athens. Lycon's sculpture had brought him important friends and anyhow that city was a place where news came streaming in from everywhere. If he had heard that the Persians were likely to cross over to Marathon...

'We have got to think, Philip. And quickly.'

He wasn't used to that. A farmer had problems sometimes and had to plan. But they usually came with the seasons, not with the speed of a hurrying boy.

They reached the house. Auntie had food ready and a cup of goat's milk. Nycilla had gone to see if Grandmother was awake yet. If so, she would be told of Philip's arrival. But not a word about why he had come – or about the Persians.

'She has aged greatly since your last visit,' Philip's aunt explained.

'She can walk only a few steps. She is very weak,' said the farmer.

At any time Philip would have been sad to hear this. In this present crisis he was full of foreboding. It sounded like a possible death warrant.

He gulped down his milk and Nycilla took him in. Grandmother looked better than he had feared. Her eyes were pale but had a glint in them. She welcomed him warmly, full of questions about his family. She even remembered old Davus.

Mercifully, she didn't ask why he had come. His uncle would deal with that tricky question. But time pressed.

He had to wait until his cousins came back from working in the fields and the problem could be discussed freely out of her hearing.

His uncle and aunt were emphatic. There was no hope of getting her safely to Athens now. Even in a comfortably padded wagon, crawling at a snail's pace along the lower track to the city, she might not survive the journey.

'And the Persians might come any day, your father tells me,' said Nearchus. 'They are famous for their light cavalry.'

'They've brought thousands of *them*,' said Philip.

'And once they're ashore they'll be galloping along that road catching up with fugitives!'

Most of the villagers would be too sensible to use that road. They would take to the hills where Persian horsemen would be unable to follow them. But how could Granny take to the hills?

Her son and grandsons might carry her bodily, struggling up those steep winding paths with their uncertain footholds. Could she stand the strain? And then the days and nights exposed on the unsheltered mountain tops? Ordeal enough to any one, even the young and healthy. Probably fatal to an old woman in her state.

They were at their wits' end. Suddenly Nycilla came up with the answer. 'The cave! Couldn't we hide her – couldn't we *all* hide – in Pan's Cave?'

5

The Cave of Pan

At once there was joy and relief on every face.

'Clever girl!' cried her father. 'Why didn't I think of that myself?'

'We could hide lots of things,' said her brother Lichas. 'If the Persians come they'll loot the whole village, probably burn our houses too.'

There was no sense in upsetting Grandmother yet. Let her enjoy another night in her own bed. But at the first sign of the invaders tomorrow Nearchus and his sons could pick up that bed, use it as a litter, and carry her up the valley to safety. Even with that burden, picking their way ever so carefully up the zigzag path, they should not take much more than an hour.

Tonight, though, there was plenty to be done. Nycilla and her mother would sort out everything that would be needed – food supplies, quantities of olive oil, both for cooking (if they dared risk a fire) and for the little saucer-shaped lamps they would need to light the darkness of the cave.

Philip joined his uncle and cousins in carrying things. Bags of flour and beans, armfuls of bedding and spare clothing, skins full of wine. Walking at a normal pace they managed two journeys each before night fell.

'We may be wasting our time,' Nycilla grumbled, though it had been her idea in the first place.

'We must be thankful if we are,' said her father.

It was Philip's first visit to the cave. Nycilla explained that it had always been out of bounds to children lest they lose themselves inside or otherwise come to harm. Also when they were small, it would have been a long way from home.

Seeing it now, he was struck by its beauty. Outside, it looked a mere crack in the limestone cliff. Once within, you realised how lofty and spacious it was, stretching on mysteriously into the very heart of the mountain.

Even now, at the end of the hot dry summer, occasional drops of water splashed down from overhead. They seemed to creep lazily down the thin shiny fingers of rock that dangled there like icicles.

'Some drops never seem to fall off,' said Uncle. 'I think they dry and turn solid and make the stalactite longer.' That was the word for these rocky icicles.

The drops that fell to the floor dried in the same way and over the years stood up spikily, like upside-down stalactites, only these were called stalagmites.

'They're beautiful,' said Philip.

'You'll have time enough to admire them,' said Lichas grimly, 'if we're all cooped up in here for days with the Persian army raging about outside.'

Between them they shifted most of their food stores and the family's cherished possessions. 'Think yourselves lucky,' Nearchus told his sons when they grumbled, 'that it's not your Uncle Lycon's workshop we're clearing.'

Next morning they were thankful they had stuck to their work so long.

Philip and Nycilla gladly obeyed her father's bidding and walked up the mountain to get a clear view out to sea. What they saw sent them racing down again.

The blue straits were dotted with black specks – at that distance looking like water-beetles – coming over from the long island opposite. War galleys and transports, there must be hundreds of them.

The foremost vessels were heading for the northern, left-hand side of the bay, where a long, very narrow, strip of land stretched out into the sea.

'They're making for the other side of the Dog's Tail,' the girl panted. 'It'll give them the best anchorage. And shelter from the wind.'

From the near side of this cape, the bay swept back towards them in a curve for five or six miles. From the water's edge to the foot of the mountains on which they were standing the land stretched out, more or less flat, for a width of two or three miles. Parts of this were marshy, particularly to the left, close to the Dog's Tail, so hardly anyone built houses there. Like Nycilla's family, most people had their homes on the lower slopes of the hills.

Just as well, thought Philip, now that the nightmare of barbarian invasion had become real!

As soon as the first Persians disembarked there would be raiding parties fanning out all over the plain. It might be death for any Greek caught there, man, woman or child. Or future slavery, which might be worse.

By the time the invaders reached the hills the people would have had time to escape inland, carrying possessions and driving their stock in front of them. The Persians might console themselves by burning empty houses, but it would hardly be worth their while to chase after the fugitives, even if their officers allowed them.

The children had no need to shout warnings as they reached the first cottages. The alarming news Philip had brought from

43

Athens yesterday had gone round the whole neighbourhood and put everyone on the alert. The rush of refugees had begun as other people had sighted the first ships and brought word of them.

Philip's aunt was making Grandmother comfortable on her bed. The men stood waiting to carry her up the valley to the cave.

'Even if she'd been fit for the journey to Athens,' said Uncle, 'I think the Persians would have caught up with us.'

Most of their neighbours, if they had no one sick or disabled, preferred to put more miles between themselves and the invaders. Some thought of shelter in the marble quarries. Others might cross the whole mountain range and make their way down into the friendly country on the other side.

It was a mercy, for their grandmother's sake, that there was this well-hidden cavern so handy for her refuge.

Once Uncle had seen her safely installed there, he became the hard-working farmer again, angry at this threat to his land and crops and the interruption to all the jobs waiting to be done.

Some it was impossible to tackle with the threat of the Persians hanging over him. Others it would be pointless to do if the enemy immediately came along and wrecked everything. But in a few days or weeks they would be gone – and the land would remain.

'And so must we,' he told the family sternly. 'Philip will keep his eyes open, but you must all be on the alert. No risks! There's so much at stake.'

There had been jobs waiting to be done. There always were. The men would work as best they could, not showing themselves to any observer at a distance, keyed up and ready for immediate flight.

'You must be our watchman,' Nearchus told his nephew. 'Sit among those bushes up on the hill. Take this horn – give us a good long blast if you see any soldiers coming this way. Then get back to the cave. Only don't let 'em see you.' He turned to Nycilla. 'You can keep him company, so long as your mother doesn't need you.'

The two of them passed the next few hours pleasantly enough, shaded and screened by the bushes, talking in low voices but never taking their eyes off the plain spread at their feet.

In the distance, beyond the long low spit of land, the moored vessels became an ever-thickening mass. Squadrons of cavalry began to thread their way across the marshy pastures at that end of the bay, but none of them swung alarmingly inland towards the encircling foothills. Rather did they keep parallel with the curving shore, dipping into the stony bed of the dried-up Charadra and pushing forward into the broad plain that backed the middle of the bay.

'This is where they're going to have their camp,' Philip whispered.

The horsemen were fanning out and coming to a halt, till they formed a thin line reaching to the water's edge. Into the space they guarded, columns of foot soldiers were now pouring as they disembarked from the ships. Tents were going up. Soon smoke was rising from innumerable fires.

Some of the figures were near enough for the sharp-eyed cousins to study them in more detail. They looked brightly dressed, in longer, more colourful clothes than the Greeks. There was less gleam of armour. Instead of splendid bronze helmets like those Philip had helped to polish for his brothers they wore dull padded headgear. Instead of bare legs, covered in front with metal greaves from the knee downwards, the barbarians wore cloth garments, often with separate legs, down to the ground.

It must be their sheer numbers, thought Philip, that had made them such conquerors. They were like giant bees, swarming over the plain.

He exchanged glances with Nycilla. They shared a sudden urge to creep away and get back to their own folk.

In the evening they went back for another look. The invaders seemed to be settling down for the night. Once darkness fell they would not stray far from the light of their camp fires, for every step would take them into the perilous unknown. By tomorrow they would be sending out foot patrols. They would search the deserted village, plunder and probably destroy the houses.

But if they saw no signs of life they might not trouble to trudge far up the hills.

'Look!' said the girl suddenly. She pointed to the southern end of the bay, where the main road to Athens vanished into the wooded foothills. The sunset flashed back from a column of crested helmets. 'Glory to Athena!' gasped Philip. The goddess of wisdom, special protector of his city, must be going to save them.

The Greeks were coming! They raced back to the cave with their good news.

6

Waiting Time

'Not tonight,' Nearchus insisted.

Those Greek troops must have come from Athens. They would have made a forced march, they must be vastly outnumbered, they would be in no state to attack the Persians, who by now were securely installed in their camp.

And 'not tonight' applied equally to any idea of making contact with the new arrivals. It was too risky in the dark. Both sides would have patrols out. The Greek camp would be ringed with alert sentries. You might be killed before you were identified as a friend.

Uncle agreed that, when dawn came, Philip would be the best person to go. As a boy he would not look too dangerous.

'And a girl will look even less dangerous,' said Nycilla. She was delighted when her father said she could go. She could show Philip the path through the woods so that he didn't need to cross the open ground. From what they had seen last night it looked as though the Athenians had halted just where the road came out of the woods at a spot called the Sanctuary of Heracles.

They started at first light, slipping through the gloom under the trees. Soon they were picking up the faint smell of smouldering camp fires. Suddenly a tall shadow moved in front of them and challenged them in a friendly tone.

'I am Philip, son of Lycon, the sculptor,' Philip answered. 'I think my brothers will be with you. This is my cousin, Nycilla.'

Even amid these thousands it proved quite simple to find Lucius and Callias.

Philip knew the company in which they served, along with the other men of their neighbourhood. Philip was soon greeting his brothers, surrounded by friendly and familiar faces.

'We wanted to go and find you last night,' said Callias, 'but nobody was allowed to leave camp.'

'And it had been quite a day,' said Lucius.

'You wouldn't have found us anyhow,' said Nycilla. She explained how they were taking refuge in the cave.

Lucius and Callias brought them up to date with the news from Athens since Philip left.

Many people had wanted to build up defences round the Acropolis and collect food supplies to stand a siege until the Spartans and other Greeks could march to their help.

Others, led by the famous soldier Miltiades, said it would be better to march out and bar the way of the invaders and stop them before they got near to Athens. Surely the Spartans would arrive in time to help?

The Athenian army had ten generals. These generals took it in turns, a day each at a time, to command the whole Athenian army of about ten thousand men. After much argument the generals voted by a slight majority to risk a battle in the open. Five of them agreed to give up their own day of command to Miltiades.

'Very sensible,' said Callias. 'He's quite the best. He knows what he's doing.'

'Too many cooks spoil the broth,' said Nycilla wisely.

The young men had to parade. 'Give our love to everybody,' Lucius called, as he seized shield and spear. 'Tell them to lie low and take care. As soon as the Spartans get here—'

He sounded confident.

When he slipped over to the cave on the following evening, the Persians had not shown much sign of moving. They were very likely resting after the strenuous time they had had in Euboea. Cavalry patrols had galloped about across the plain, they had plundered and pulled down some empty huts, but they had kept their distance from the Athenians on their wooded slopes.

'Lucky for us,' said Lucius.

'Shouldn't the Spartans be here?' Nearchus asked.

'That's the trouble.'

Pheidippides had got through to them with that message. He had covered that stupendous run of 140 miles and got back with the answer. It was rumoured that Pan had appeared to him on the road and given him super-human strength. Certainly from that day the god Pan was more popular in Athens than ever before.

Unfortunately the Spartans were just then celebrating an important sacred festival in honour of the god Apollo.

'Very religious people, the Spartans.' Lucius sounded bitter, almost disgusted. 'They said they had to obey the holy law. They must wait till the moon is full before they can march over to help us.'

By themselves the Athenians were hopelessly outnumbered. The strength of the Persian forces – judging by all those ships – might be 30,000. It was a wonder that they had not already advanced against the Athenians.

Lucius thought they did not fancy attacking heavily armed infantry in a strong position. They hoped to lure them down into the open plain where the Persian cavalry could make rings round them.

Next day brought sudden hope. Looking up into the mountains Philip caught the welcome glitter of armour. It was as though a giant metal snake was winding its way down from the skyline. Could it be the Spartans after all?

The newcomers however turned out to be from the loyal Athenian ally, the little city of Plataea, over in the west above the Gulf of Corinth. Plataea had sent its entire army, only a thousand men, but a great encouragement.

'Every man counts,' said Lichas. He and Nycilla's other two brothers went over to the Athenian camp, with a handful of young neighbours who came down from the hills.

They had no arms but their knives and hunting spears. 'If the fighting starts,' Lichas pointed out, 'there will soon be shields and weapons scattered around. And the men they belong to may be in no state to pick them up!' His sister shuddered. 'We'll soon equip ourselves,' he assured her. 'We'll be all right, you'll see.'

They were accepted as light infantry. Their knowledge of the ground might be useful. Philip wished he was big enough to join them, but had to admit that he would be of no use.

'One thing worries me,' said Lucius.

'What's that?' someone asked.

'Five of our generals have given up their turn to Miltiades. Tomorrow's his last day to command. *He's* far our best chance of winning. What will happen if he has to hand over command to someone else?'

What would tomorrow bring? Not the Spartans, anyway, thought Philip.

7

The Day of Destiny

Miltiades was spoiling for a fight. There was no doubt of that.

But Miltiades was no fool. How could he march out and attack a Persian army perhaps three times as big as his own?

The Persian cavalry were the greatest threat. Apart from small mounted patrols, riding to and fro across the plain, they had not so far been much in evidence. But they were there all right. Their horses could be seen in the distance, grazing in the wide marshes.

They could be rounded up and mounted fast enough if the Greeks came down on to the open ground. Miltiades must be well aware of that. He had experience of Persian fighting in other places and other wars. And he had no cavalry of his own to throw against them.

Philip and Nycilla took their usual early walk next day on the higher slopes above the cave. Their elders encouraged them. Everyone wanted to hear if there was any sign of action round the bay. If the restless young were happy to make that steep climb no one would discourage them.

'If only the Spartans would come,' said Nycilla for the hundredth time.

'They won't,' said Philip. 'Not today.'

Every night he scowled up at the moon and calculated. Even when the Spartans were free to start, even though they were famous for their forced marches, they could not compete with the speed of an Olympic runner.

The cousins mounted a crest which suddenly gave them a wider view of the bay.

'Look!' the girl cried excitedly. 'There are no horses! Where have they gone?'

The marshy pastures were almost empty. Philip looked to the right, bracing himself for some alarming sight – the massed cavalry suddenly in movement against the Greek position. There was not a horse to be seen.

'They must be in the ships!' exclaimed Nycilla. 'Yes, I can see some being led on board!'

Philip swung round. She was right. There seemed to be great activity along that spit of land. Files of horses were led up gangways into the transport vessels. Some ships were already well out into the bay. Sails were being hoisted. A screen of war galleys, with their long banks of oars, was strung out across the open sea.

'They are giving up,' said the girl hopefully. 'They can see it's no good. Oh, Philip, it's almost too good to be true!'

'It *is* too good to be true. The camp's still there. Look, the soldiers are all there. And they're forming up. Thousands of them.'

She stared down, mystified. She hadn't always listened, as Philip had, to the endless discussions of the men during the last day or two. She had found it so boring. But now she was desperate to know what was going to happen. She begged Philip to explain.

He did his best. If the Persians could not tempt the Greeks down into the plain, their famous cavalry was no use to them. But while the two armies glared at each other at Marathon, the city of Athens was left defenceless. If the Persian cavalry sailed south along the coast they would be able to land, practically unopposed, within a mile or two of their main objective.

'Can Miltiades get back to Athens in time to stop them?' she asked.

'Not with the rest of the Persian army on his heels! I don't see how.'

It seemed hopeless. It would be suicide if the Greeks at Marathon turned their backs on an unbeaten army almost three times the size of their own.

Philip turned his gaze back, despairingly, to the Greek encampment in the Sanctuary of Heracles. Despair turned instantly to disbelief.

The troops were already on the move. But the first marching column was not wheeling south along the road back to Athens. It was turning into the Marathon plain and heading straight for the Persian camp.

'There's going to *be* a battle,' he said.

They stared down, speechless, as they tried to take in the scene.

Only Argus, nosing about happily as usual, had no idea that history – perhaps tragedy – was about to be made. His keen questing eyes were only at their knee-level. Perhaps he couldn't even see what was happening far below. And what would his dog's mind have made of it if he could?

The Persian host was already ranged in order of battle in front of their camp. Their backs were to the sea. Some of their fleet, both war galleys and transports, were lying off shore, but there was no sign of any horses being disembarked again. They were no doubt in the other ships that were already far-off specks, heading for Athens.

Probably, thought Philip, the Persian commander was not unduly worried. He had no cavalry against him. He had such superior numbers of infantry that they could surely cope with the Greeks alone.

That superiority was more obvious than ever now that Miltiades was forming up his own battle line. It was so thin by comparison with the dense mass facing it. And so *short*. Both to right and to left the barbarians extended further.

Miltiades had realised the danger of this. His own left and right wings had been stronger than his centre. Now they were both thinning out to lengthen the Greek line until it faced the Persians from end to end. More files of men were leaving the centre and marching away to one flank or the other.

For some reason the general seemed determined to keep those wings up to strength. Was he taking chances, Philip wondered, making his centre so weak? What if that barbarian horde smashed its way straight through?

'Ought you – ought you to go back?' he asked Nycilla.

'How can I?' she answered fiercely. 'My brothers are down there, just as yours are.'

'I was only thinking – if the worst comes to the worst—'

'Well?'

'If our people have to fall back – some of them might come up here – with the

Persians close behind them—' He groped for words. How could he explain to her the horrors in his mind? Those murderous barbarians would be scouring the mountainside for fugitives!

'I'd run then,' she promised.

'You must. And so will I. We mustn't let them see us – or the way we go. We must get down to the cave – but we mustn't lead *them* to it.' That would be the final horror. Even their grandmother wouldn't be spared if they found her.

The Greek line was moving forward now. They had no idea where their brothers were. Not on the extreme left wing, thought Philip – that position, he imagined, would have been given to the Plataeans. They might be anywhere else in the battle line.

'They're shooting!' Nycilla whispered.

Clouds of arrows were flying from the enemy archers. The Greeks continued their advance without faltering. Those helmets and breastplates and shields were giving the protection they were expected to. A trumpet sounded. As one man, the glittering ranks broke into a run.

A great shouting arose, a din of clashing weapons, as the two armies met.

'I can't bear to look,' cried the girl in a strangled voice.

'We're pushing them back!' Philip shouted joyfully.

Argus just paused, his puzzled head cocked, mystified by the medley of noises from below.

Philip had been only partly right. The Plataeans seemed to be doing well. So were the Athenians at the far end of the line. But in the centre, as he had feared, the enemy were breaking through. It was the sheer weight of their numbers, which Miltiades had been unable to match.

A few minutes ago the two armies had faced each other as thick, straight parallel lines. Now those lines had crashed together. They were merging into a shapeless mass, quivering in conflict, curving outwards or deeply dented, according to the way men pushed forward or had to give ground.

Miltiades must have known what he was doing when he kept his two wings strong. They were pushing back the men facing them. With their longer spears and their defensive armour they exploited their advantage. And, remembering no doubt the instructions given them, they were not wasting time to chase after Persian fugitives but were circling round in orderly fashion to take the enemy's triumphant centre from behind.

'It was wonderful,' he told the family afterwards. 'Like a crab's claws!'

'Look!' cried Nycilla. She herself could bear to look now. 'They're running away! They're running into the sea!'

The Persian centre had turned to meet the surprise attack on its rear. There was a mass of struggling humanity, a blend of yells and howls of pain and clashing weapons. But some of the barbarians were already in terrified flight, many of them splashing into the shallows and wading out to find safety in the vessels lying just off shore.

It was getting to be little better than butchery. It was hard to believe afterwards. But a little later, when Philip and Nycilla knew it was safe to run down the mountainside on to the battlefield, they saw evidence that for the rest of their lives they never forgot.

That little stretch of plain was strewn with bodies.

Hundreds – indeed, as it turned out, thousands. Almost all barbarians. The Greek casualties, dead or wounded, were already being picked up and tended by their comrades. But there had not been many.

No one was troubling much about the invaders. They littered the ground, their long Asian garments soaked with blood. Their shorter spears had been little use against the longer Greek ones. Their wickerwork shields had been a poor protection compared with the strong ones of their enemies.

Philip and his cousin rushed past them – sometimes over them – with no more than a shuddering glance. They saw Lucius and Callias and rushed over to them. Callias had a flesh wound which Lucius was trying to bandage. Nycilla made a tidier job of it.

'Have you seen my brothers?' she asked anxiously.

'Lichas picked up my shield and asked to borrow it,' said Callias. 'They were all right then.'

'We must find them,' said Philip, seeing the look on her face.

There was no danger now. The Persians had piled into their ships and fled. To Nycilla's relief they quickly ran into her other brothers and found them untouched, but of Lichas there was no sign. They all joined in the search with growing alarm.

Suddenly Philip spotted the Gorgon's head. His brother's horrific shield scowled at them from a little heap of bodies. 'Lichas must be somewhere near,' he shouted. Hope and fear mingled in his voice.

Argus quickly removed the uncertainty. He leapt forward, tail wagging furiously and sniffing among the fallen Persians. They heard a feeble voice from somewhere: 'Good dog!'

They found Lichas flattened under an immense Persian. 'This brute tried to kill me,' Lichas explained as the young men released him, 'but I got him first.' He was not really wounded and was quickly himself again once the crushing weight was removed.

The casualties had been remarkably light. One hundred and ninety two Athenians had been killed. That number was later laid to rest in a special memorial tomb on the battlefield where they had died. Though the Persian dead had to be picked up and buried, it was done with less ceremony, for there were six thousand, four hundred of them.

On that day, however, there were more urgent things to think of. Thousands of other Persians had escaped in the ships. They would by now be sailing after the vessels that had earlier started for Athens with the horses.

Trumpets summoned the men on the battlefield to an instant roll call. They were told then that after a meal they would have to face an overnight march back to Athens. The danger to their city was still great. Because of his slight wound Callias was excused this, and he went back with Philip and their cousins to the Cave of Pan.

It was a brilliant scene, that noisy family gathering. The torches, the little oil lamps twinkled and danced as their reflections were caught in the graceful fingers of ice tapering from the arched roof of the cave. Everyone seemed to be laughing and shouting at once. The nightmare had ended. It was a long time before anyone could think of sleep.

An eventful week was almost over. Two thousand Spartans arrived a day or two later. They had come through Athens and brought reassuring news – the Persian fleet had duly arrived there but so had Miltiades and his victorious troops after their forced march. The Persians had put out to sea again without even attempting to land.

The Spartans inspected the battlefield, expressed compliments all round, and went home to Sparta.

Philip went back to Athens with Callias, and their father was able to finish the statue of Pan. People declared it was quite remarkable. A year or two later he made one of his niece as a nymph. And everybody thought Nycilla quite remarkably beautiful.

Glossary

The Acropolis A fortified hill top at the centre of Athens. This was the most famous part of the city, where the important religious and secular buildings were located.

Cavalry Soldiers who fight on horseback.

Greaves Pieces of armour worn from the ankle to the knee.

Gorgon A monstrous woman in Greek mythology who had snakes for hair and turned anyone who looked at her into stone.

Infantry Soldiers who fight on foot.

Litter A bed or seat with two long poles on either side, on which people would carry a single passenger, especially someone sick or wounded.

Nymph A goddess or spirit of nature living in areas of natural beauty and traditionally regarded as a beautiful young woman.

Parthenon The chief temple of the goddess Athena built on the Acropolis at Athens between 447 and 432 BC. The most famous surviving building of ancient Greece.

Pedestal A base for a statue.

Persia An ancient empire that stretched from the eastern Mediterranean Sea to Pakistan.

Sparta An ancient Greek city-state famous for its military.

Strait A narrow channel of the sea linking two larger areas of sea.

Tunic A loose, sleeveless, knee-length item of clothing worn in ancient Greece.

Historical Note

The ancient Greeks lived in the lands around the Mediterranean Sea, reaching from Turkey to Italy. Ancient Greece was not one large empire but was made up of different city-states. The states guarded their independence and sometimes even went to war against each other.

The city-states were ruled in different ways and each had its own government, laws and money. However, they traded with each other and usually grouped together if one of them was attacked by a foreign army.

Although ancient Greek cities themselves were generally smaller than cities today, they also controlled the surrounding countryside. For example, Athens ruled over the region of Attika, which was fertile and rich in natural resources such as silver, lead and marble. This helped Athens to become one of the largest and most powerful states.

Athens was named after Athena, the goddess of wisdom. In 508 BC a new form of government was invented in the city and Athens became the world's first democracy. This term comes from the Greek word *demokratia*, which means 'rule by the people'. Any person with full citizen rights could take part in public debates and vote to decide how the city was run. This group of citizens was known as the Assembly. However, by no means all the population were invited to attend. A 'citizen' was defined as a man who was born in Athens and who owned land there. Women, foreigners and slaves were not considered citizens and so could not take part in government. The Assembly met every ten days on a hill called the Pynx. It made decisions on every aspect of Athenian life: from street cleaning and taxation, to whether the city should go to war.

Another important city-state was Sparta, which was ruled by two kings and a small group of elders. Sparta was a military state with a very strong army. All Spartan boys were trained to be soldiers. So when Athens found itself under attack from the Persian Empire, it naturally turned to Sparta for help.

The Persian Empire controlled Asia Minor, Lydia, Judah, Mesopotamia and Egypt, and was a significant threat. When Darius the Great became Emperor he wished to expand his territory and conquered Macedon, just north east of Greece. In 490 BC he set out to conquer Greece itself, starting with Athens. Darius and his many troops landed in the Bay of Marathon, about 25 miles from the city.

The Athenian army was greatly outnumbered by the Persian one, so it sent out a messenger named Pheidippides to run the 140 miles to Sparta to ask for reinforcements. Messengers were also sent out to the other major city-states. However, these were unwilling to send troops as they were jealous of Athens' growing power. Then Pheidippides returned from Sparta with its reply – the Spartans were celebrating a religious festival and their troops would not arrive for nine days. Athens realised it was on its own.

On the face of it, the Athenian troops stood little chance; they were outnumbered about three to one by the Persians.

However, the Athenian troops were well trained and also had one major advantage – the Athenian general, Miltiades, had once been a soldier in the Persian army and knew its tactics. The Persian force was poorly organised and expected individual, hand-to-hand fighting. Under Miltiades' command the Athenians made a sudden mass charge at the unsuspecting Persians. The Persians were encircled by the Athenians and were almost literally driven into the sea.

After the battle, the Persians counted 6,400 dead soldiers and many more captured. The Athenian dead totalled only 192. Supposedly the messenger Pheidippides ran the 25 miles back from Marathon to Athens to announce their victory. According to legend he reached the city, said, 'Rejoice, we conquer' and fell dead from exhaustion. This famous story has given us the name of the modern marathon race, which is the same length as the distance from Marathon to Athens.

The Battle of Marathon is perhaps the most important battle in Greek history. Had the Athenians lost, all of Greece would most likely have ended up under the control of the Persian Empire. The Athenians saw the battle as one of their greatest achievements. From then on they began to think of Athens as the centre of Greek culture and Greek power, and this is the way people still perceive ancient Athens today.

Map of Ancient Greece

ACROSS THE
ROMAN
WALL

THERESA BRESLIN

The year is 397 AD and life in Roman Britain is getting dangerous...

Marinetta is a Briton, Lucius is the nephew of a Roman official. When they first meet they hate each other. But when marauders cross Hadrian's Wall they are forced to work together.

ISBN 0-7136-7456-3   **£4.99**

A Candle
in the Dark

ADÈLE GERAS

The year is 1938 and the world is poised
on the brink of war...

Germany is a dangerous place for Jews.
Clara and her little brother, Maxi, must
leave behind everything they know and
go to England to live with a family they
have never met.

ISBN 0-7136-7454-7 £4.99

CASTING THE GODS ADRIFT

GERALDINE McCAUGHREAN

The year is 1351 BC and a new pharaoh
is ruling Egypt...

When Tutmose and his family arrive in
Pharaoh Akhenaten's new city, they are
delighted to be taken under the ruler's wing.
But the pharaoh's strange ideas about
religion will change life for them all...

ISBN 0-7136-7455-5 £4.99

DOODLEBUG SUMMER

ALISON PRINCE

The year is 1944 and World War II is not over yet...

There have been no air raids for a while, so Katie's family don't sleep in the shelter any more. Then one night, Katie wakes to hear a strange, loud noise, followed by a big explosion. The Doodlebugs have arrived...

ISBN 0-7136-7579-9   £4.99